CW00429446

BOTH
PUBLISHING

Published in 2020 by BOTH Publishing.

The author asserts their moral right to be identified as the author of their work, in accordance with the Copyright, Designs and Patents Act, 1988.

Copyright © Steven Savile 2021.
All rights reserved.

This book is sold subject to the condition that no part may be reproduced, distributed, or transmitted in any form or by any means, including photocopying, recording, or other electronic or mechanical methods, without the prior written permission of the publisher.

A CIP catalogue record of this book is available from the British Library.

ISBN - 978-1-913603-02-1
eBook available - ISBN - 978-1-913603-03-8

Printed in the UK by TJ Books Limited.
Distributed by BOTH Publishing.

Cover design and typeset by Chrissey Harrison.

Part of the Dyslexic Friendly Quick Reads Series.

www.booksonthehill.co.uk

Sherlock Holmes and the Four Kings of Sweden

Steven Savile

Other dyslexic friendly quick read titles from BOTH publishing

The House on the Old Cliffs

Ultrasound Shadow

The Clockwork Eyeball

Anchor Point

At Midnight I Will Steal Your Soul

The Breath

The Man Who Would Be King

Sherlock Holmes and the Four Kings of Sweden

The Bernadotte Chambers

The Old Town

Stockholm, Sweden, 1930

It was a lonely walk into the spotlight at the centre of the auditorium. The room was filled with ghosts and draughts, though it was impossible to tell which was which as they brushed up against me. To amuse myself I tapped out a message with the tip of my cane as I crossed the bare boards. It was short and sweet. I wondered if any of the brilliant minds gathered to listen would notice I'd just given them a clue to the real secret of the lecture?

Holmes had decided against attending. Something far more interesting, he assured me, had caught his attention just an hour before he was meant to join me on stage and simply could not wait. He refused to enlighten me, promising I would find out in good time.

"It is with great pleasure, I present to you, Mister Sherlock Holmes and his associate, Doctor John Watson."

I gave them a moment for the polite ripple of applause to subside. My hosts were nothing if not polite, which I am assured is a Swedish trait.

I set my cane down beside the

lectern and nervously shuffled the sheaf of papers I'd meticulously prepared for my talk. Even after all this time I was uncomfortable addressing an assembly, though in this case, I confess, my nerves were due in equal measure to who was listening in the banked seating and the fact that a good many of them would not be able to understand a word that came out of my mouth.

"Thank you," I said, "Thank you. As you can see, I am... ah... diminished. That is to say only half here, or as we Brits are wont to say, not all there," I offered a self-deprecating smile to the gallery. "My name is Doctor John Watson. Some of you may be familiar with my stories," I paused, allowing for a few murmurs of agreement to return to me. "Though

I suspect you are here out of curiosity rather than any great desire to listen to an old man talk about his famous friend."

Holmes had picked some thirty names to attend our first lecture here in the icy north – at the invitation of the Justice Minister, Georg Bissmark himself, who was seeking to establish a School of Detection much like the many we had lectured at across the world, sharing Holmes' methods with the most promising criminal minds of two generations now – and dispatched a plain black invitation to each of them with the address and time of my lecture embossed in gold foil on the front and an individual message to each on the reverse.

There was nothing random about their selection. Each of the thirty men had come to our attention during our investigation into a curious fellow who called himself the Magister, which loosely translated to the Master of Science, and was derived from a form of the word teacher. It was a curious name, befitting a most curious investigation. One most worthy of study, and hence the subject of my inaugural lecture.

A disembodied voice up in the gods said something I didn't catch. Swedish is a most peculiar language, more fitting to the trill of a mynah bird than the mouth of a man.

"If you would humour me, beneath your seats you will find an envelope. Would you be so kind as to open it?" I gave them a few seconds to retrieve the envelope and empty its contents.

There were several reproductions of key evidence and testimony inside, but for now I wanted to focus on the newspaper. "The Riddle of the Four Kings," I said, giving the signal for the lights to come up. A few confused murmurs greeted the sight of last month's *Svenska Dagbladet* headline.

"We have all read the papers, Doctor Watson," another voice heckled.

"Why are we wasting our time with this? It is just a stupid story, nothing more," another said.

"On the contrary," I opined. "On the face of it, what we have here is a curiosity, one in which the king has been sighted in four different cities, each of them several hundreds of miles apart, from Lund in the south, to Gothenburg on the west coast, Stockholm itself, and moving north, Uppsala, on the same day, an undoubted physical impossibility and yet in each instance crowds of people attest to having seen His Majesty acting distinctly out of character. One eye witness we could assume to be mistaken, but fifty? Five hundred?

"We cannot merely dismiss the phenomenon as either mistake or prank. We could, of course, ask His Majesty," I said, looking up towards the Royal Box, letting his royal presence sink in, "but for now, humour me. Let us consider, how could such a thing happen?"

"It can't," the same speaker said, adamant in his refusal to believe the impossible.

"Good. Yes, you are of course absolutely correct. It cannot happen. The principles of the physical universe stand. An object cannot exist in multiple locations simultaneously. So we eliminate that from our thinking and evaluate the remaining alternatives to deduce the truth.

"One obvious possibility is that the reports are false. Lies. But for that to be true we must consider upwards of a thousand eye witnesses across the country being complicit in the same lie, which is unlikely to say the least."

"Actors?" someone asked.

"Excellent, now you are thinking. Indeed, some form of paid shill is indeed a viable solution. It would mean locating seven men bearing a passing resemblance to the king, and each putting on a performance, deliberately wanting to be seen. To be remembered.

"Worthy of note, too, then is the fact that these reports all make reference to the king behaving out of character. For a student of deductive reasoning an answer like this begets more questions. First and foremost: why? Motivation is a fundamental aspect in understanding the criminal mind. Without it, we lack a clear picture of the crime. So, why would seven kings all act out of character? What possible reason could they have to be seen acting out?"

"To discredit His Majesty," a voice called.

And there it was, the underlying reason for our visit to this inhospitable land.

"Very good, yes, to discredit the king," I agreed. "And the moment that kind of thinking becomes a part of our deductive process it changes everything. That story ceases to be tomfoolery and becomes something entirely more sinister because there must be a grander - darker - scheme at play."

There were grudging murmurs of assent from around the chamber.

There was a nugget of something there that defied easy understanding.

It was precisely the kind of thing that attracted my friend to a case and why he had been so keen to take up Bissmark's invitation.

We had only been in the country for a fortnight and in that time I had amazed at the culinary horrors the locals called food – mainly fish, preserved in a manner that doesn't bear thinking about, and the distinct lack of fresh vegetables, something I must admit I took for granted thanks to the easy abundance of them back home – and the sheer cold.

The lodgings we had been afforded included a quite ingenious use of one to help preserve the other; the pantry, or skafferi as they called it, was constructed in such a way that there was an air vent built into the outside wall allowing the sub-zero air to fill it, keeping the food cool, extending its life. It was so simple in its logic and construction you could not help but admire the Swedes their industry.

"As I am sure you have surmised by this point, your invitation to this inaugural lecture was no mere coincidence. Each and every one of you is vital in some way to the solution of this most vexatious plot. Indeed, over the next few hours, with your help, I intend to unmask the criminal mastermind hidden within our ranks.

"What better way to prove the value of deductive reasoning and underline the importance of our techniques to truly understanding the criminal mind."

There were gasps of astonishment, which I had expected. I made a study of their faces, but not a man betrayed anything that might have been read as guilt.

"We should begin, I think, at the beginning, which would be our first encounter with the name the Magister."

~

The snow was deep but far from crisp and decidedly uneven, the ruts in the slush caused by the constant flow of foot traffic.

A tram rumbled away around a distant curve in the road, unperturbed.

I followed my companion on a circuitous path around the spreading puddles of slush. Holmes walked with singular purpose, eyes fixed on some invisible point in the middle distance. He did not stop for man nor beast until we arrived at the door of the theatre.

The bill posted beside the door promised mind-bending feats of illusion and mentalism from the Danish mystic, The Great Andersen. I was unfamiliar with his name.

"What in the blue blazes are we doing here, Holmes?"

"Following the crime," he said.

"What crime?" I asked, feeling, as I did so often, about a dozen steps behind my companion.

"All in good time, my dear Watson. All in good time."

He paid with a crisp five kroner note, purchasing two seats towards the back of the house. As we followed the usher's torch to our seats I noticed a peculiarity of the seating arrangement that, in retrospect I think wonderfully illustrates the Swedish personality. The audience gathered in seats around the middle of the house, leaving plenty of spaces at both the front (where the view was restricted but you were close enough for the actors to spit on as they enunciated) and the back (where the view was panoramic, but the sound was less than ideal). They were the Goldilocks People.

The word they used to describe this phenomenon, lagom, has no literal translation into the King's English. It is not enough, or satisfactory, or any such Latin derivative, and dates back to the time when their ancestors passed the drinking horn around the fire, each man supping the perfect amount for the horn to make it all the way around the fire.

As an ethos it was deep-rooted in the Swedish psyche. In every situation there was a Goldilocks solution that was just right.

Feeling rather pleased with my deduction, I took my seat. There was no one in any of the three rows immediately in front of us, which afforded us a wonderful view of the stage.

I waited, wondering what point Holmes was trying to prove, through a series of tricks that were competent if not awe-inspiring, and more often than not included some rather obvious gimmick if one took a moment to consider what you were being shown as opposed to what you were seeing.

Finally, Andersen called for volunteers and three men took to the stage. I watched with fascination as he proceeded to hypnotise them and by turns planted trigger words and suggestions in their minds that had them participating in all manner of parlour tricks. "This is what you wanted me to see?"

"Indeed, Watson. What did you make of it?"

I wasn't immediately sure how to answer that. "You believe we have stumbled upon a crime involving mesmerism?"

"There is a very strong probability, yes."

"A crime in which weak-minded fools

are put into some sleep-state and made to act against their moral compass? I'm not sure I believe it."

"Did I say anything about a weak mind? I did not. In fact the reverse is far closer to the truth – the fiercer the intellect, the greater the self-control, the more susceptible a subject is likely to be to mesmerism. Entering a hypnotic trance requires intense concentration. Note I said trance, it is not sleep, another great fallacy. The subject is actually in a heightened state of concentration, again quite the reverse of sleep."

"And this has some bearing to a case I know nothing about?"

"It does indeed, Watson."

He presented me with a folded up

front page from a week old broadsheet. Above the fold the headline read: The Riddle of the Four Kings. I read through it quickly, my initial instinct to dismiss it as rubbish, but as I folded the page again, I said to my companion, "And this is the true reason for our presence here, not the opening of a school of detection?"

"Our visit has a dual purpose, my friend. Note the four locations Gustav was allegedly sighted. What do each of them have in common?"

"Aside from the fact they played host to a monarch who was noted to act most peculiarly?"

"Yes."

"I must confess, my knowledge of our host country is wanting. Enlighten me."

"Each city is well known for its academia. Lund is the site of the country's oldest university, Gothenburg, and Uppsala, whilst Stockholm hosts three of Sweden's most prestigious schools, Kunliga Tekniska Högskolan, the Karolinska Institute and of course the university."

"Strong minds," I said, seeing the link, as tenuous as it currently was, but what on earth makes you think there is a crime here?"

Holmes handed me a second item. It appeared to be a ransom note, words cut from articles from the same newspaper to spell out some threatening message I could not read. "What does it say?"

"We know your secrets. Do you want

the world to know them?"

"And this was addressed to the king?"

Holmes nodded.

"Someone is blackmailing the king? That is hard to fathom. I cannot begin to imagine what manner of secrets these must be."

"Bissmark was not forthcoming when I asked about their nature, other than to say they are most personal, and scurrilous lies with it. Whatever they are they run deeply enough to have caused genuine concern at the Royal Palace, though. Initially I was inclined to dismiss it, as all people of power and influence attract those of a troubled disposition at some time during their lives, but coupled with the sightings of these faux Kings, I believe we are seeing the opening gambit in what will be a greater crime to come."

"And you have a plan?"

"We must find ourselves one of these imposter kings. Without proof of wrongdoing we are merely clutching at broken straws and hoping to stumble upon a whole one."

"Then that is what we must do. But where to begin?"

"We have already begun, my friend," said Holmes. "Mister Andersen here has performed several engagements across the country, first in Lund, then Gothenburg, Stockholm and Uppsala."

"That is an eerily familiar route," I observed with a wry smile. My friend, as ever, was one step ahead of the game.

"Where should we be looking next?"

"He has been invited to one final engagement in Sweden, a private function. One might go so far as to call it by Royal Command."

"Oh, now that is interesting," said I.

I picked Karl Andersen's face out in the audience.

The mystic looked nonplussed. He would, I believe, prove to be a worthy opponent across the gaming table. He studied me with quiet fascination.

I was more than a little interested in watching his face as I presented my first surprise of the evening.

"The mind is a curious thing," I told my audience. "One would not think it possible to so influence a soul that he would completely lose all inhibitions and all sense of self, but with the right skills, such trickery is akin to magic," I said. "Kent Nylander? Would you be so good as to make yourself known?"

My request was greeted by a shuffle of feet and the scrape of the man's chair going back. Even now, Nylander bore a striking similarity to the man up in the Royal Box. It really was uncanny, but even so, there were many subtle differences that marked the two men as different, some as simple as posture and bearing, others ingrained from lives lived most differently. But for a moment his appearance was enough to fool enough of the audience into thinking that they were seeing double that there were audible gasps from a few.

"Now, as you can see, Kent is a fairly unremarkable man save for his passing resemblance to His Majesty. In fact, Kent is one of our faux kings. He was responsible for the reports generated in Uppsala."

I watched Andersen's face most closely, but if there was guilt within his mind he did well to hide it.

The next few minutes promised to be most interesting if Holmes' supposition was correct. We had watched the mesmerist's show and made specific note of some of the cues he used to trigger the more peculiar behaviour.

I crossed the floor to the front row, dealing out a number of small cards, each with a statement from Andersen's show written neatly upon them. I did not trust my grasp of phonetics to do anything other than mangle the language, so I asked, "Would you be so kind as to read out the line written on your card?" to the first man. He looked puzzled by it, but did as he was asked.

"Som är vid dorren?"

Who is at the door?

Immediately Nylander's head whipped around, and tongue lolling slackly he began to bark. His barking lasted a full twenty seconds. It was a cheap parlour trick, but given our surroundings a powerful example of just how easily a man's mind could be influenced if you knew how.

"And now you," I said to the second man.

"Du är I brand."

You are on fire.

Nylander greeted this one by slapping his arms and chest vigorously, trying to beat the invisible flames into submission.

No one was laughing this time.

The man fell to his knees, seemingly trying to pull the hair from his scalp.

"Tillräckligt," I said, the one word I had committed to heart. *Enough*. That was how Andersen had ended the theatrics on stage, and it worked here.

I nodded to the third man in the front

row who had Nylander hopping on one foot for half a minute, then dancing an uncontrollable dance as he believed the floor beneath his feet to be quicksand. And on it went down the line, each new humiliation reinforcing the point that Kent Nylander was not in control of his own actions.

"Now, I don't believe it is as simple as saying 'Kent, behave like a king,' and him doing it, but as I hope I've just demonstrated, such an imperative would account for the reports of the king acting out of character, as each and every one of us have a different idea of what it takes to be a king. But it does nothing to answer the question of: *why*?"

"Curious," Holmes said.

Something had obviously caught his attention. "There is a story here of a day before the four sightings of the faux kings which suggests Gustav was seen in a small mining town north of Uppsala – Sala. I had thought nothing of it as there were no conflicting reports that day, but I believe we may be looking our mesmerist's first attempt at manipulation, a dress rehearsal for the main event. Look."

He handed me a copy of the newspaper that I could not read beyond picking out key words like king and Sala. "What am I looking at?" I asked.

"A throwaway line, Watson, nothing more, but I believe to be telling.

Gustav, like most Nordic nobles, is an accomplished hunter. That is well documented, but the final line suggests the elk evaded its hunters and the royal party returned home empty handed."

"That is tenuous, Holmes. Perhaps it merely knew the land better than the hunting party?"

"Perhaps, but what better way to test your deceit than to replace your subject in the most familiar of environments and see if any note his sudden loss of skill?"

He had a point, it would have been a most efficacious test of the mesmerist's substitution, if that was truly what was happening here. What better dry run than that?

"I still don't see what Andersen stands

to gain from this game of kings?"

"Power, inevitably," Holmes said. "Wealth more immediately. You control a monarch, you control more than merely the trappings of royalty. This land is not like our own, my friend, far from it. Here there is a ground swell of distaste for the blue bloods, a growth of social democrats and liberals who would be free from the tyranny of kings."

"You think this is an attempt to bring down the monarchy?" I said, aghast.

"It is not so long ago that a peasant uprising saw the nation teetering on the brink of outright revolution akin to the events of Russia. The Conservative government fell to a coalition of socialist and liberal parties greatly influenced by the teachings of Marx and Engels. The situation called for desperate – and radical – changes to stave of the collapse of a way of life, and the upshot was a huge reduction in political powers from the absolute authority of the king, effectively transforming the monarch into a figurehead. It is a small step from that to a Republic."

"All it would take is a disgraced king," I agreed, following his inescapable logic.

"And here we find ourselves with a king harbouring secrets."

"Secrets," I added, "that are known to others."

"Are barely secrets at all," Holmes finished. "It behoves us to travel north, my friend. I believe we will find at least one solution to this sorry affair in the mining town."

"Who in their right mind would want to be a king in days like these?"

"Indeed," said Holmes, thinking.

It was in Sala that we first stumbled across the Magic Circle and a man who called himself Thurneman.

It wasn't his given name, indeed it did not take long for my friend to deduce that it was in point of fact an anagram, a clue to his true nature: manhunter.

Between the capital and the mining town the landscape was one of trees, trees and more trees. Every genus of hardy evergreen clinging to their colour as they battled the elements to live up to their name.

Our train pulled into the station an hour before midday. The sun was bright on the snow, the air several degrees colder than it had been back in Stockholm when we'd embarked upon our journey a few hours earlier. My first impression of the town was one of almost fairy tale cuteness, the architecture in keeping with my imaginings of Grimm's Bavaria.

We moved slowly, neither of us young men anymore. The locals were wrapped up against the cold, features hidden behind layers of scarves and thick woollen coats. Even so, they left a trail of foggy breath in the air behind them as they went about their business.

Our first port of call was with the hunt master who had arranged for the king's unsuccessful outing in the local forests. His house was a crooked blue building where the old timbers had twisted so far out of skew the only thing holding it upright was the buildings on either side.

The narrow cobbled street was one of a few survivors from a huge fire that had scoured the area around the town square, laying waste to three hundred years' worth of history in a huge blaze. We opened the gate which opened onto a courtyard where the man's horse grazed beneath a barren apple tree. The poor animal looked wretched.

Our intrusion was greeted by the manic bark of a terrier intent on making sure we came no further. The hunt master followed the baying chorus to greet us on the threshold. He babbled something at us that was frankly unintelligible, but Holmes took it in his stride and countered with a slow precise phrase he'd committed to memory. I heard the word English, or something very much like it, in there and assumed he was asking the man if he spoke the language.

The hunt master shook his head and proceeded to say something, but it sounded different to my ear. Louder, slower, as though by talking to us like children – or simpletons – we'd suddenly grasp what he was saying simply because it was loud enough and slow enough to make sense to us.

Holmes was adept with languages, and had a good grasp of Latin and a smattering of German and French. I had even heard him utter a few words of Mandarin. There was, as so often, no limits to my friend's ferocious intellect.

He repeated the same question, though this time there was no mention of English. He was asking the man if he spoke German, earning a slight shrug as though to say a little. It was enough for Holmes to work with. They proceeded to mime and mumble question and answer, somehow making each other understood. It was quite the performance.

I found my concentration drifting, and my gaze moving around the cramped room. It was surprisingly warm, given the chill outside. A log fire was banked up in the corner, and combined with a ceiling so low Holmes had to stoop, it generated considerable heat. I noted a photograph of the royal hunt on the windowsill and crossed the room to study.

The man in the picture, I realised quickly, was a southpaw, while Gustav himself was very much right-handed. Little things betray so much, I thought. A riding crop in this case. The man in the picture wore a tartan scarf over his mouth and nose to shield him from the elements. I noticed the same tartan scarf hung on a hook behind the door.

Through the window I noticed a second building across the inner courtyard that looked to be a mirror of this one, single storey, with a cellar arrangement and low sloping red clay roof. It appeared to be some sort of workshop.

After a lull in the interrogation, the

hunt master led us across the narrow yard to the second house, and inside to a room where all of the accoutrements of the hunt were stored, including, I noted, the brass horn the king would have used to sound the charge.

Holmes studied the instrument for a moment before hanging it back on the hook and turning his attention to something else. If I hadn't been paying attention I would have missed him palming the brass mouthpiece and slipping it into his pocket. He made a show of asking a handful of questions, but I could tell he wasn't particularly interested in the answers. He'd found whatever it was he'd come for.

We left the hunt master with directions to a public house two streets over, but not before my companion asked whether he might borrow the scarf to protect himself from the biting wind. He had noticed it, too.

There is no better indicator that you are a visitor in a strange land than the sky above your head with its familiar constellations of stars in unfamiliar positions. I noticed the distinctive arrangements of Ursa Major and Minor which back home would have been a little above my right shoulder were away over my left. It was the most disconcerting change the world could ever offer. I remember still the confusion the first time I looked up at the utterly wrong skies above Afghanistan. What I wouldn't have done for a little of that desert heat now.

Despite the fact that the walk took

less than three minutes our body temperature dropped by half, to the point where I felt sure the blood would freeze in our veins.

The tavern was welcome respite. We made something of a grand entrance, trying to beat the warmth back into our bodies as we crossed the threshold and took up seats beside the fire. We were approached by a lithe blond serving girl who, I assume, asked us what our fancy was. Holmes answered in German. After a moment's hesitation she nodded, mentally moving tracks to the unfamiliar second language, and left us to settle in beside the warm fire while we waited for our food.

There were half a dozen diners in the taproom; men with the calloused hands of physical labour. My first thought was that there was nothing menial about such tasks in a hostile clime such as this.

Holmes put the mouthpiece on the table top between us.

"What am I looking at?"

"See for yourself."

I picked up the fluted piece of brass and turned it over in my hand, back and forth several times. I noticed some obvious wear around the edge where lips and teeth would have come up against the metal, and was about to dismiss it once again as something I wasn't seeing, until I noticed the thin traces of white powder-like dust on the inside of the hole. I raised it to my nose and sniffed, but there was no discernible scent, and then proceeded to lick the tip of my finger and went to dab the tiniest sample of the white dust on the tip of my tongue.

"I wouldn't do that if I were you." Holmes stopped me short.

I looked at him askance.

"What is it?" I asked.

"Proof that our king was not who he purported to be," Holmes said. "A sulfosalt. I thought perhaps given our proximity to a silver mine, it was evidence that our imposter spent some time in the mine shafts beneath us, some sort of residual from the mining process, but the hunt master assured me the mines have been disused for the better part of twenty years. Now I believe it to be a trace residue from the arsenic that was used to poison him. Dead men do not make the most reliable of witnesses."

"If he was poisoned where is the body?"

"We have an endless expanse of forest out there," Holmes said. "Acres upon acres upon acres. Plenty of room to dispose of a corpse."

"What now then?"

"Now, like our investigation thus far, we go to the dogs." He held up the tartan scarf. I understood immediately what he had in mind, but I must confess I was in no great rush to go back outside.

We could not very well hunt by night, so we resigned ourselves to a long evening of inactivity.

We could not have been more wrong in our assumptions.

Holmes used the Rikstelverket phone booth in the main square to place two calls through the operator, one back to the police headquarters in Stockholm, summoning urgent assistance - including a translator - and the other the master of the hunt, informing him that we would like to book a private hunt for first light.

I watched him through the window, listening to the sing song conversation of others in the pub, not understanding a word. I had never felt so isolated in my life, if honest.

The logo on the telephone kiosk was of a lightning bolt, or more precisely two lightning bolts, contradicting the notion that lightning did not strike the same place twice. The girl brought our food, fairly basic fare of meat and potatoes, overly salty but a marked improvement on the sour herring we'd had the day before.

Holmes looked most frustrated as he strode back across the gravelled square to join me. Without a word he withdrew his pipe from the folds of his coat and proceeded to fix himself a smoke. He did not say anything until he had exhaled his fifth deep draw of smoke, and then it was merely to inform me that reinforcements would be with us before dawn.

We took lodging in the rooms upstairs,

one of six vacant rooms the landlord let to transient workers, but contrary to my expectation, rather than sleep Holmes arranged the bolsters beneath the blankets to give the illusion of our sleeping bodies, and leaving the door unlocked, retreated to a second unoccupied room to wait out the night.

I thought, for a moment, I heard scratching within the walls. Rats. I shivered at the thought, but of course given the hostile climate the rodents would seek refuge just like anyone else. I confess to thinking his precautions were a mite paranoid, but some two hours later, in the darkest part of the night, when two gunshots rang out in quick succession I changed my mind.

He raised a hand to still me.

I was without my trusty service revolver. Indeed, our only weapon was my cane, though Holmes could easily transform it into a deadly weapon and I was no slouch in the martial arts myself, but I would always rather things didn't come to that if it could be helped. The mind is the key to set us free, as the great Houdini used to say. I heard footsteps on the landing, and in our room angry shouts of puzzlement and rage. Three voices, so we were outnumbered.

"How did you know they would come for us?" I whispered, barely daring to breathe.

"I did not," Holmes admitted, "but once I placed the call with the master of the hunt, Thurneman, I knew there was no little risk in doing so I would tip our hand should Thurneman be on cahoots with our blackmailers."

"Which he obviously is," said I.

"More than that, I have gravely misjudged the threat. We were to be murdered in our beds, not to be run out of town."

"What now?"

He put a finger to his lips. The plan was obvious, we wait. Outside our second room I heard a brief scuffle as the invaders argued over their subsequent actions. Gunshots cannot go unanswered, even in a small town like this. Those two shots would have been heard, and the police would inevitably respond sooner rather than later. Our best course of action was merely to wait because their best course of action was to flee the scene of the would-be crime.

I counted silently to thirteen before I heard the first footsteps on the stairs, going down.

Still we waited.

Eventually I heard the outside door slam, and it occurred to me to wonder how our would-be killers had found their way into the public house unhindered in the first place. The door had been left unlocked, pointing the finger at someone, most likely the landlord himself, and turning this into a grand conspiracy indeed.

The police arrived as we emerged from hiding. I was surprised to see the familiar face of Stefan Lindblad, one of Bissmark's special detectives, who had driven up from the capital during the night to lead the investigation and serve as our translator. The man, in his early fifties, wore a grizzled expression of determined confusion, not unlike Gregson or Lestrade back home. He issued instructions to his officers quickly, barking out the orders with a semaphore of movement as he sent them hither and yon, before turning to face use. I don't mind admitting it was good to see a familiar face so far from home.

"Mister Holmes, Doctor Watson," he said, "Would one of you mind telling me what is going on here?"

"Murder," my companion said. "Or at least a very good attempt at it. You will find two very dead pillows in the room upstairs."

"Shot clean through the feathers," said I, much to the policeman's confusion. "A little English humour," I told him.

"Come sunrise I believe we shall find an actual corpse," Holmes said, and now there was no trace of humour.

Lindblad took a small black leather-bound notebook from his pocket and turned over a couple of pages to a blank one. I noticed several doodles on the reverse; the man obviously had a most febrile imagination. He proceeded to jot down notes as Holmes ran him through what we knew, or at least suspected.

Rather than wait for morning proper, the detective had us lead him through the empty snow-covered streets to the crooked blue house of the hunt master, and hammered on the gateway door with enough force to wake the dead. They didn't, however, raise Thurneman.

Lindblad gestured to a couple of his subordinates and stepped away from the door so that they might kick it down. It was no easy task, but eventually the wood yielded, splintering around the lock, and we were inside.

It was obvious that the place had been vacated in a hurry; the remains of a half-consumed supper were still on the table, the chair Thurneman had been sitting at on its back in the middle of the floor where he had cast it aside. The bakelite telephone was off the hook. Holmes strode across to it, hung up the handset and then lifted it again to get the attention of the operator.

"Who was the last person called from this phone?" he demanded, and when the operator didn't answer in any way he found satisfactory, he thrust the handset towards Lindblad and told him to ask the same question.

The answer was not unexpected, being one Thomas Allwin, the owner of our lodging house. We had our smoking gun. A conspiracy was unfolding around us. Rather than rush back to the pub to arrest Allwin we took a moment to search the hunt master's home looking for anything of significance to our investigation.

The main house was filled with curiosities that I do not mind admitting made me most uncomfortable, including several examples of amateur taxidermy gone slightly awry. The glassy eyes of the various creatures truly did seem to follow me around the room as I made my search. I discovered his journal stuffed down the side of a battered leather armchair.

Lindblad translated the epigram for us:

> "To take another man's life
> is no crime, it only means a
> change in the physical state,
> since the soul is immortal and
> lives on in something else, an
> animal or a human being. To
> take from another human being
> only means a change in the
> state of possession in this life."

"Cheerful thought," said I.

"It belongs to the teachings of Raya-Yoga movement from the Far East," said Holmes.

The frontis page bore a most peculiar symbol, a triangle with a circle within and a circle without. I saw the same image repeated throughout the book, with text beside it I could not read.

Lindblad offered a translation. "The triangle represents the three true members of the church, the circle within, symbolises the inner circle of trusted members, and the outer circle represents those who are not truly a part of the church but can be called upon if needs must."

"And there is a roster of names?"

"No, but there appears to be a draft of a contract, which would suggest a paper trail exists to be found."

"Which is something," said I, but Holmes was not so easily appeased. He stalked out of the room. The outer door slammed in his wake. I saw him cross the inner courtyard, but instead of entering the parallel building on the other side, he pulled up storm doors that lead down to the cellar and a moment later disappeared from sight.

I followed him out.

By the time I arrived he had lit a gaslight and stood engrossed in the study of what can only be described as a wall of occult madness; each symbol was scratched into the plaster with a knife blade, gouged deep into the calc. I saw again the symbol I would come to associate with the Magic Circle, but there was so much more, too, things recognisable from the work of Madam Blavatsky, Crowley and other charlatans. Holmes was engrossed by them. I found the images more repulsive than fascinating.

He nodded three times in quick succession, digesting everything the wall had to tell him, and then he was off, moving at a loping run, his long legs carrying him up the narrow wooden stairs into the room above, where he snagged a ring of keys off a hook, and then he was out the door.

By the time I caught up with him a baying chorus of hounds filled the night.

I hadn't even seen the second gate inside the small courtyard when we had been here earlier in the day. It opened onto kennels where the hunting dogs were kept. Holmes had them gathered around him as he knelt, holding out the tartan scarf the imposter king had worn for the hunt. I didn't need to ask what he was playing at, once the dogs had got the man's scent he released them. It was all we could do to keep up with the half a dozen hounds as they tore through the maze of narrow streets.

"How could they possibly have the scent already?" I laboured a few steps behind my friend, but ahead of Lindblad and his fellows who were slower to react to Holmes' burst of frenetic energy than I was, but then I'd had a life time of getting used to his peculiarities – so much so they hardly felt peculiar to me at all these days, they were just Holmes being Holmes. He loved the chase. The energy.

I gestured for Lindblad to hurry up before the dogs disappeared out of sight. We rounded the corner onto the main square, only to see the dogs already merging with the night-dark alleys that led away on the other side, past the old church and the stately park. I could hear rather than see the dogs now as we struggled to match their pace.

Without torches we were at the mercy of the moon, but curiously the night was not all dark, but rather illuminated by the snow on the ground. It was a curious trick, but I was grateful for it just the same. The ground was treacherous under foot, but we made our way through the park, our eyes fixed on the dark skirts of the forest that loomed up ahead of us.

The dogs disappeared into the trees.

We struggled manfully to keep up, drawn on by their ragged barking as it changed in tenor, becoming more aggressively frantic. They'd found whatever it was they were looking for.

We followed a narrow track which ran parallel with the run-off river from the silver mine. The moonlight reflected on the frozen water. Back when the mine was active they would have had someone out breaking the ice to ensure the boats could progress unhindered. The dogs, I saw, had crossed the frozen water and circled around an empty patch of ground, digging with their paws. I knew what we were going to find before they finished digging it up.

A hand.

"Detective Lindblad, could I put upon you to describe what happened next in your own words?" I called up into the gods.

"'*Vist*,' the Swede said, then caught himself and corrected the words in his head. "Of course. We approached the area where Mister Holmes was already on his knees, digging at the loose dirt with his bare hands. The dogs had found a shallow grave in the woods."

"And what – or rather who – did you

find in the grave?"

"The king," the policeman said, to shocked gasps from the assembly. "At least that is how it first appeared, though as the dogs clawed at his face their claws tore at some of the prosthetics that had been used to better shape his face and enhance the physical similarities."

"So it wasn't the king?"

"No, and to be honest it did not look much like him. I could not for the life of me imagine how it could fool someone in his inner circle."

"Fascinating," said I, turning my attention to the royal box, "is it not, your majesty?"

"Most," the king said. "If not a little macabre to think of one's own body in a woodland grave."

"I would imagine so," said I. "Thankfully it is not something the majority of us have to contemplate." I turned my attention back to Lindblad. "So what happened then? Could you talk us through it?"

"It took some time to exhume the body," the grim Swede said. Thankfully he spared us most of the details. "It was only when it was out of the ground that I noticed something weighing down the right pocket of his top coat. A room key from Allwin's, the public house in the centre of the town."

"And the room in question?"

It was the room we'd taken refuge in when Thurneman's thugs had tried to kill us the night before, and put Thomas Allwin right at the heart of the mystery.

Up until that moment I'd been content to consider him something of a rube in the play, but he was no innocent, that much was becoming abundantly clear.

Lindblad's men turned the room upside down, ignoring the landlord's protestations. I studied the man as he made a nuisance of himself; he was well dressed, dapper even, in pinstripe trousers and a snug-fitting waistcoat, though his boots were incongruous, heavy miners steel toe-capped affairs. They found nothing, but as I studied the man, so too did Holmes, and his eye was far keener than my own.

"You," he said to the landlord, "are going to confess your role in this whole sordid affair."

Allwin gave no indication that he understood a word of it, but as my friend moved a step closer, raising a finger as though trying to gauge the wind direction, his eyes darted furtively to the left, towards the dresser in the corner.

Lindblad's men had already turned it out so I knew there was nothing to be found it there, yet for all my certainty the fact the man's gaze instinctively drifted that way had me puzzled. I took it upon myself to cross the room, then pull open the first drawer, but the man did not so much as flinch, same with the second and third drawers even as I turned them out and turned them upside down. Nothing.

So it wasn't the dresser that had him anxious, but something in its vicinity.

Outside, the sun was rising.

That was another thing that took some getting used to. We were well into the morning but the sky outside was still essentially grey and not much lighter than it had been in the middle of the night. The sun was finally beginning to break through the holes in the cloud, offering something approaching daylight. That fact, and that alone, was the only reason I caught the pinprick of light through the flock wallpaper as I turned away from the dresser, defeated.

It took me a moment to register what that tiny pinhole of light *meant*.

I knocked on the wall above the

dresser. My fist was greeted by a curious hollow reverberation of plasterboard and space behind it. "It's hollow," I said.

"Of course it is," the landlord objected. "There's a room right on the other side – *your* room." But that didn't match up to my memory of the building.

I rushed out of the room, counting out the paces in the hallway, then unlocked my own room, measuring the distance to the wall. It did not add up. I repeated the pattern of knocking on the wall, moving along the wall as I tried to sound out any differences in the echoes that came back to me. There was definitely some sort of cavity between the rooms.

I pushed and probed at the wall trying to find whatever mechanism would trigger the access, but there was no tell-tale click to match my endeavours, which could only mean the access panel was in the royal suite. I chuckled at the notion of ascribing anything so grand to this fleapit and went back through to repeat the search.

Holmes watched my efforts in silence, and only after waiting a good five minutes for me to properly humiliate myself, pointed at the ceiling. It took a moment to register, but of course I should have known he was already one step ahead. Lindblad dispatched two officers to investigate, and a moment later we heard movement in the wall before us.

"Rats in the walls," Holmes said, and I remembered hearing the scratching as we waited for Thurneman's goons to pay their nocturnal visit.

A moment later the wall swung slowly inwards and we were face to face with Lindblad's two coppers. The space between the walls was actually a narrow room, with a chair, gas lamp and a few conveniences to make waiting less of a chore.

"What in the world?" I said, more to myself than to the others, but that did not stop Holmes from explaining it to me.

"We know your secrets. Do you want the world to know them," said he.

I caught his gist immediately.

This room was the source of the salacious lies Bissmark had been so quick to dismiss. The fact that it was a bedroom was all the explanation I needed. "There is a woman, no doubt?"

"We will have to ask Master Allwin, as I suspect he will have procured her services for the imposter king to make sure that events unfolded the way his paymasters required."

The dapper man shook his head, a look of genuine fear on his face.

He obviously understood every word that passed between us.

"I can't tell you," he said. Not I don't know. I can't tell you, which of course was a matter of choice.

"Now, now, Master Allwin, you quite obviously can tell us, your lips move quite adequately, and there is a tongue in your mouth. The only thing preventing you from telling us is the fact you are labouring under the misapprehension that you have a choice in the matter."

"Please. Please. I can't." He backed up a step, then another, and another until his back was pressed against the wall. He didn't stop shaking his head the whole time.

"All we need is a name," Holmes said.

"You don't understand; it will be the death of me."

"How very melodramatic," said Holmes. "I understand your co-conspirators will look most unfavourably on such a betrayal, but as their own liberty is but a few hours longer than your own, I can assure you they will not be in a position to make good on any threats."

"They won't need to," Allwin said, "It's

in here," he pressed two fingers against his forehead. "He put something inside me... if I betray him I am finished." He was shaking. Clearly he believed what he was saying. "I made a promise. I am bound by it. If I break my vow, I will die. There is no way out. He made sure of that. I am bound to them. Please. You cannot make me tell you. There must be another way." He looked around the room frantically.

I was sure in that moment that he was looking for something that might be used to end his own life.

Holmes said something. It took me a heartbeat to register that it was one of the trigger phrases we'd heard the Great Andersen deliver to much amusement, and in response the landlord dropped to his hands and knees and scratched around on the floor like a chicken in search of feed, pecking his forehead at the room's bare boards over and over.

"Mesmerism," I said, in disgust.

"Look at me, man," Holmes said, his voice deep, regular, the rhythms of his words slow and easy.

Allwin had no choice but to do as he was told.

"You cannot force a man to act against his better nature. I cannot plant some seed in your brain that would make you act against the basic urge of self-preservation. To think otherwise is preposterous." Which was easy to say, but harder to prove. The man looked unconvinced. "I want you to listen to my voice, concentrate on my words, I'm going to put you into a trancelike state and remove the imperatives put in place by Thurneman. To prove that you are free to talk, I will repeat the trigger that had you thinking you were a chicken a moment ago. You will be free of the subconscious imperative, and likewise free to talk. Understood?"

We watched as Holmes focussed Allwin's attention, and within just a few moments had him submersed in a deep fugue state, awaiting instruction, neither awake nor asleep. Holmes' voice was gentle, reassuring, but far from removing all of the supposed triggers, he merely told the man he would no longer feel the need to act like a chicken when he heard that word.

"When you wake you will no longer be afraid of Thurneman, he cannot hurt you or make you hurt yourself, do you understand me?"

"Yes," Allwin said.

"Very good. I am going to count backwards from ten, and when I reach one you are going to tell me the name of the girl who was used by your confederates to falsify evidence against the king. Do you understand me?"

"Yes."

"Very good," said Holmes. "Ten...Nine..."

There was a woman – there is always a woman. In this case she was the only woman in my audience. I invited her to tell her story.

Her name was Maria Nordqvist, and in every way imaginable her life was utterly unremarkable save for one; she had been a honey trap for a man she believed to be her king.

She rose awkwardly, smoothing down the bustles of her best dress. Her flaxen hair had been braided and put up in hoops. Her face was striking if not exactly pretty, her nose too sharp, her cheeks too sculpted to ever be called beautiful. She was distinctively Scandinavian in appearance, slim, narrow hips accentuated by her skirts. She coughed once, clearing her throat.

"In your own time, my dear," I reassured her.

Unlike Allwin, she didn't speak English, so one of Lindblad's men interpreted for her, repeating her story every couple of lines.

"I was told that to betray their cause meant certain death – at my own hand. They proved they could manipulate me into doing what they wanted, simple parlour tricks I could not resist, taking control of my body. All it would take was a word, Thurneman promised, a single trigger word, and I would not stop until I had ended my own life. And I believed him."

"What made you change your mind?"

"Mister Holmes."

"Would you mind explaining how?"

"He put me in a mesmeric state and removed the trigger. You can tell me to bark like a dog, nothing will happen now."

A few of the men in the gallery laughed, but there was an edge to the atmosphere now, everyone waiting with baited breath for the truth to finally be laid at their feet.

"Would you care to tell us what happened in that room?"

She nodded. "I was forced to entertain a man while they watched from their hiding place, taking photographs."

"And these photographs were of a lewd nature?"

She nodded, colour rising in her cheeks. I did not wish to push her further or cause unnecessary embarrassment, but I had one last question for her, and needed the woman to spell it out so there could be absolutely no doubt. "Could you identify the man?"

"I should hope so," she said, earning a nervous laugh from somewhere up in the gods.

"Let me rephrase that: would you be so kind as to make the man's name known to everyone here."

"I can do better than that," said she, pointing a finger up in the direction of the royal box. "That's him, there."

She'd picked out the king from all the faces in the room, as I'd known she would. I had seen the photographs. The quality was poor, the images blurred from lack of light and the peculiar arrangement they'd been forced to manufacture to better focus on the bed through the pinhole in the wall, going back to the first very basic principles of photography.

The images were barely more than blurred suggestions, crude in both senses of the word, but good enough for the purpose of extorting the king. Bissmark had known that from the moment the envelope landed on his desk. It didn't matter if the man in them was Gustav or some imposter, once they were seen they could never be unseen and people would make up their own minds as to the veracity of the images, meaning he'd be damned before sundown.

Holmes was right in his thinking that there was a growing groundswell of opinion in this country that wanted to see the Bernadotte's humbled.

"There is only one thing that remains," said I, "And that is to present to you the mastermind behind this whole sorry affair and see that justice is served."

That was a cue, and my man up in the rigging earned his keep, focussing the full beam of one of the theatrical spotlights on a seat right in the middle of the audience.

The man looked up, perturbed. His face was heavily lined, each deep crease well-earned if his bearing was anything to go by as he slowly eased himself up to his feet. Holmes had been most adamant that this final reveal posed the single greatest risk to the house of cards our case was constructed from, but as this was nothing if not a learning experience for the watchers', failure was not the end.

"I think you will find yourself mistaken, sir," the man said in impeccable English. "I am innocent of any and all of your accusations. Indeed, I am as innocent as your good self, as I have an unbreakable alibi."

"And that would be?"

"Why, you, Watson. And might I congratulate you on a truly fascinating examination of what was a most vexatious investigation." I knew that voice better than I knew my own, and as Holmes slowly peeled the first layer of prosthetic from his jawline, changing the entire shape of his face, I could not help but marvel at how well he had disguised himself in plain sight. "There remains but one thread to pull that we might unravel this entire mystery."

"And that would be?"

"The identity of Mister Thurneman, who, as Inspector Lindblad has highlighted, does not and has not ever existed. He is a ghost."

"But there is no such thing," said I.

"Indeed," Holmes agreed. "The name puzzled me for a while, until I realised it was nothing more cunning than an anagram, made more complex by being in English as opposed to the man's native tongue. When you have the key it is not difficult to crack, Thurneman is of course a Swedish sounding rearrangement of the word manhunter, a clue to the nature of the man himself, who arrived mysteriously in the town a matter of a month or so before the first sighting of the imposter king. This is the man behind *four* imposter kings, who has practiced the art of deception and misdirection. My first thought was that his true identity was actually that of the mesmerist the Great Anderson, a man, who in turn appears to have no past. But what would a stage magician stand to gain from blackmailing a king?"

"Power," said someone in the audience to his left.

"Influence," said another, this time from behind Holmes.

"Money."

"The unholy trinity," Holmes agreed. "But it wasn't until I had studied the itinerary for the man's tour that I realised the same man was in the audience at every single performance."

Now he had my attention.

"And who might that be?" I enquired.

"Why, the king, of course. Each show was a gala performance. And at three of the shows theatre workers reported that the mesmerist had been offered an audience with the king. So I asked myself a question: what could a king want with a man who made a living from parlour tricks? It took some thought, but it was something that Watson said that set me to thinking about the world this king finds himself living in, and how it is a thankless place where his throne is being stripped daily of its power and influence. Then another question occurred to me: what happens in a game of kings when the monarch truly does not want to be king at all?"

"Are you saying the king was behind his own blackmail? That makes no sense."

"And yet it is the truth, the grand crime to extort the king himself, a crime that just a few moments ago you dismissed as a stupid story, was never more was half of the tale. Misdirection, like the magician's art. The true crime was nothing more than a king looking for a way to leave his throne, is that not the case, Your Majesty?"

The man's brow furrowed, but he

offered no answer. No defence. No denial.

"Why not merely abdicate? Cede the throne to one of your sons?" I asked. There were three, each of an age where they could rule with something approaching wisdom.

"Abdication does not solve the problem of a civic uprising and an outdated form of rule, does it? The aim, the end game, is a bloodless revolution, if you like. The king giving his country back to its people. Look at how many lives were lost in the October Revolution and the Civil War that broke out in its wake. What man of good conscience would ever want to inflict that kind of suffering upon his people, even if those people appear to have no love left for him? It must be sorely tempting to want to simply disappear. And who better to help with that than a renowned mystic," said Holmes. "A man whose entire life is built around illusion. He helped you plan the whole thing, did he not?"

The king nodded. There was sadness in his eyes. Regret. How must his life have crumbled for it to come to this?

"What about the body in the woods?" I asked. "The first imposter king. Surely you aren't claiming the king was somehow responsible for the murder of a man?"

Holmes shook his head. "Not directly. He most certainly never gave the order. In this case there was never a first imposter, was there, Your Majesty? There were only the two men who bore a striking resemblance to you, and then you yourself, acting out a part. That was you in Sala, was it not? And then again in Uppsala and Stockholm. Who better to play the king than the king himself?"

Gustav nodded, once, solemnly.

I looked from him to the woman as the realisation she had truly bedded her king sank in, my mind wrestling with the reality Holmes was offering up.

"So if it wasn't an imposter king, who was it?"

"Why, Watson, is that not obvious? It was the king's man, or as he styled himself, the *manhunter*. Thurneman had served his purpose. He could not be allowed to walk free, though, as the risk of him telling what he knew was too great."

"Someone still killed him," I protested. "Murder is murder."

"Indeed, but we will never know who. The corridors of power are murky at the best of times. These are not the best of times in this land, my friend. Even so, there isn't a man alive who would willingly betray a king he had gone to such lengths to protect, so we must content ourselves with knowing that we have done what we were brought here to do, assembled as fine a group of minds as could be hoped, and I think in this one lesson given passing fair introduction to the idea of deductive reasoning and why one should always look beyond the headlines and their sensationalism for the truth that lies at the very heart of the matter."

It was difficult to argue with that, but then it was always difficult to argue with Holmes as he had the frustrating habit of being right all the time.

THE END

About the Author

Steven Savile is a bestselling British fantasy, horror and thriller writer. He lives just outside Stockholm, Sweden having emigrated in 1997.

His published works include *The Memory Man*, *Coldfall Wood*, *Glass Town*, *One Man's War*, *Parallel Lines*, and numerous short stories in magazines and anthologies.

He has written for Games Workshop, *Primeval*, *Stargate* and *Doctor Who*.

Steven was a runner-up for the British Fantasy Award in 2000 and again in 2010. He has been published in a dozen languages and sold more than half a million copies of his novels and stories worldwide.

Also by Steven Saville

The Memory Man

Parallel Lines

Glass Town

One Man's War

Coldfall Wood

... and more.

We would like to thank everyone who
made this project possible,
via the Kickstarter and outside of it.

Specific thanks goes to:

Aaron Armitage

David Parker

Ross Warren

More dyslexic friendly titles coming soon...